The "Little" House

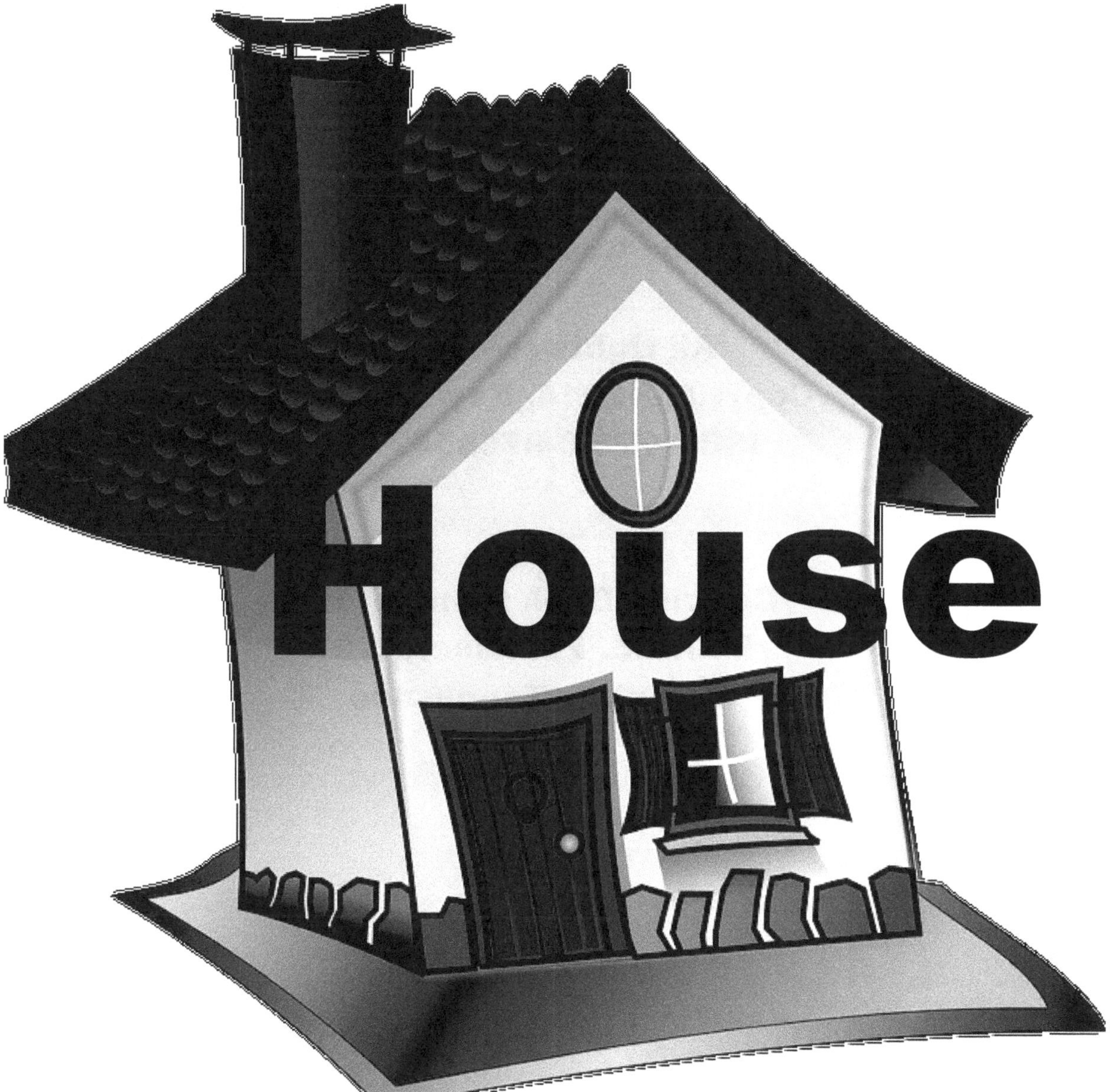

The Little House - A Coloring Book

Story by Dasia Carter

M.O.R.E. Publishers
Memphis, Tennessee

The “Little” House

A Short Story Submitted
by Dasia Carter

ISBN 978-0-9758549-8-3

Coloring Book Concept by
M.O.R.E. Publishers CO
Memphis, Tennessee

Once

there

was

a little

house.

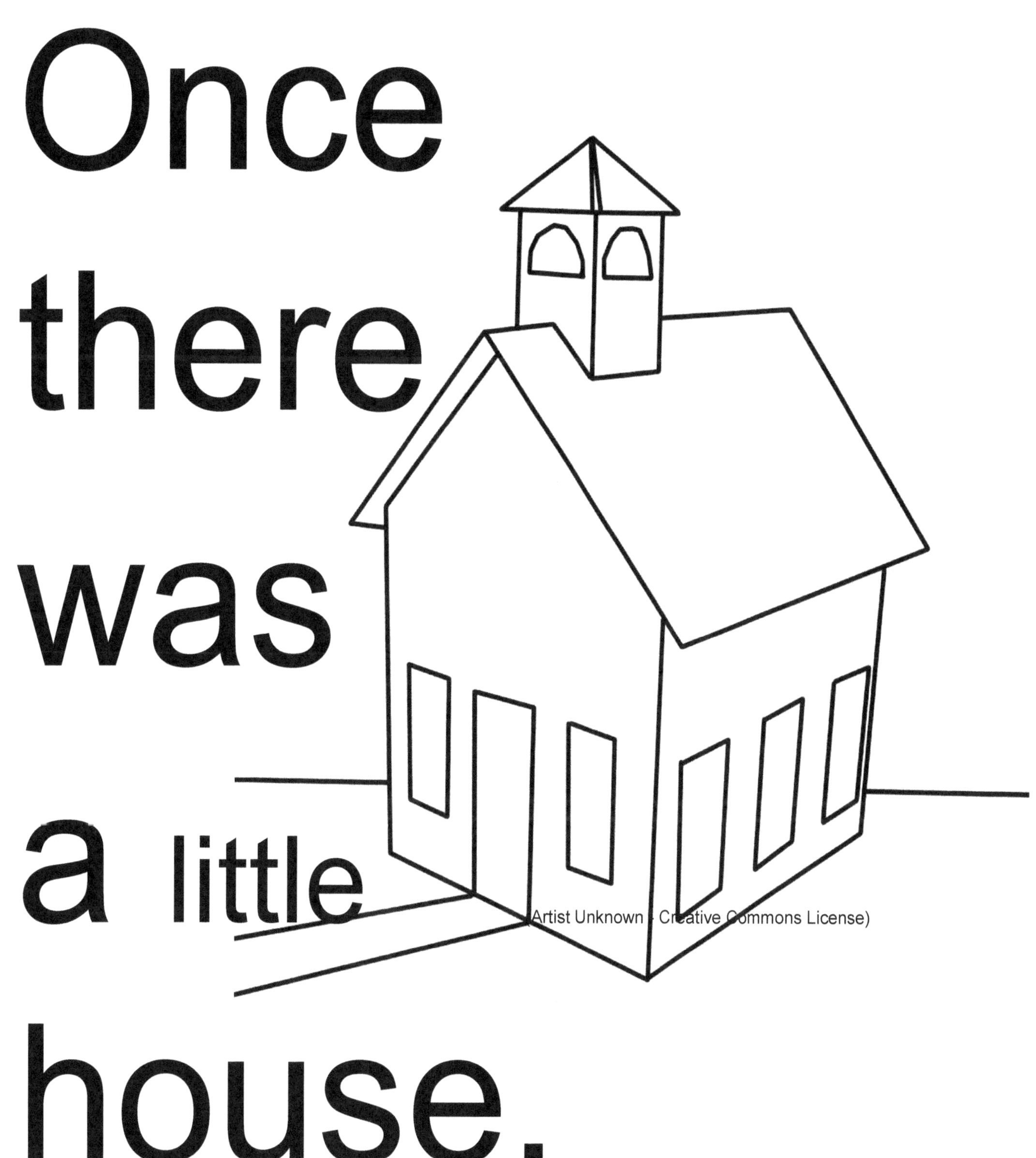

The little house loved

(Artist Unknown - Creative Commons License)

the town where she was made.

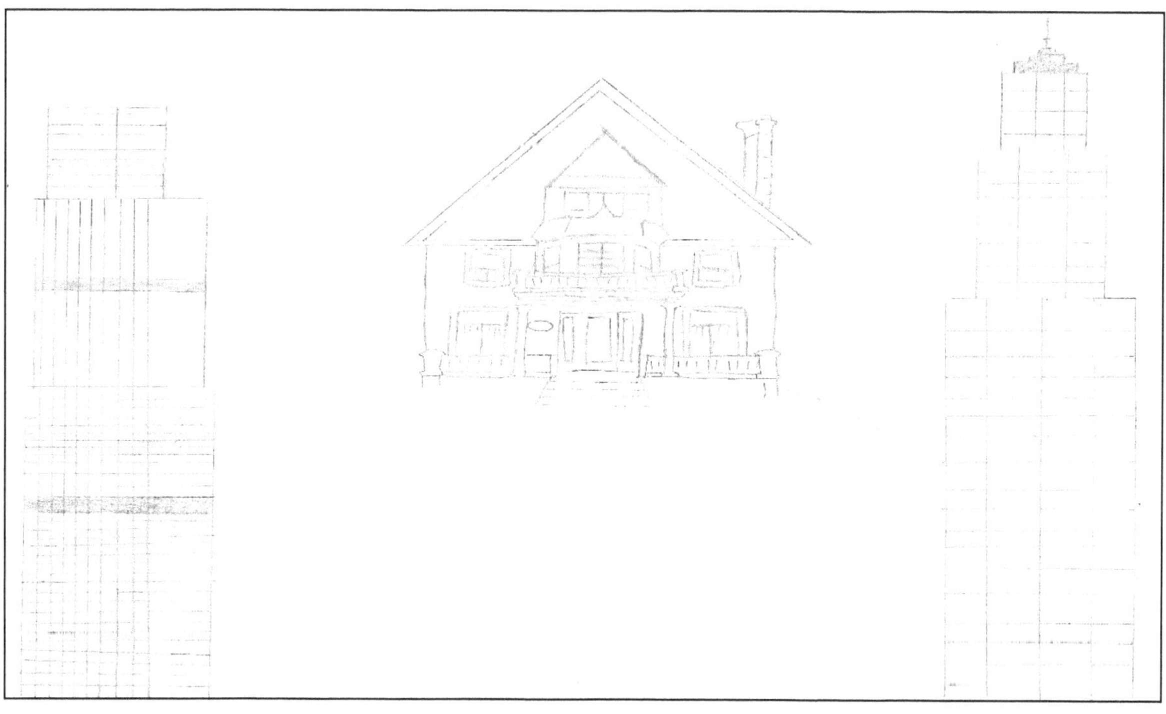

Terry L. Holt, artist (Memphis, Tennessee)

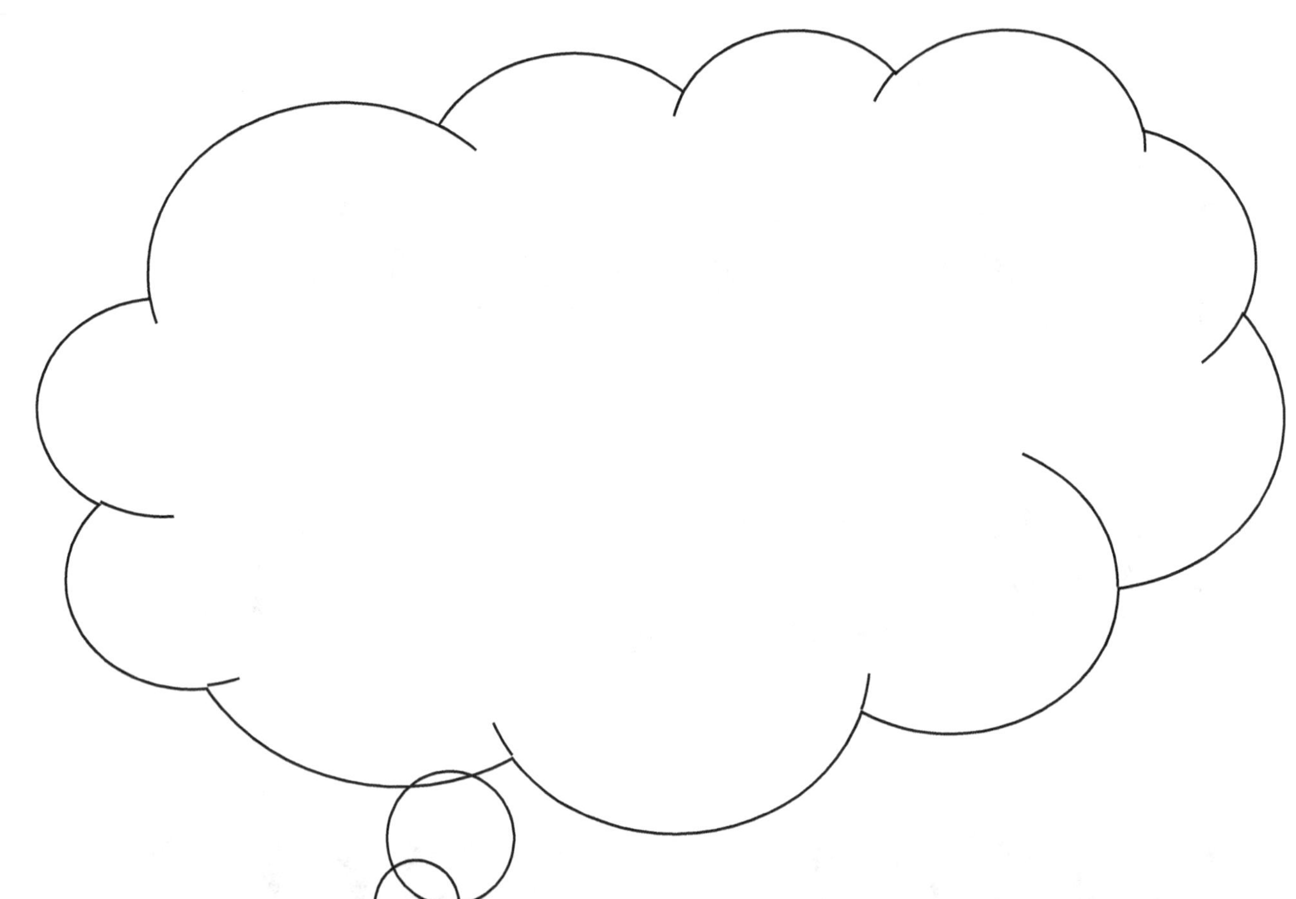

But she always wondered,

“What will it be like in the city?”

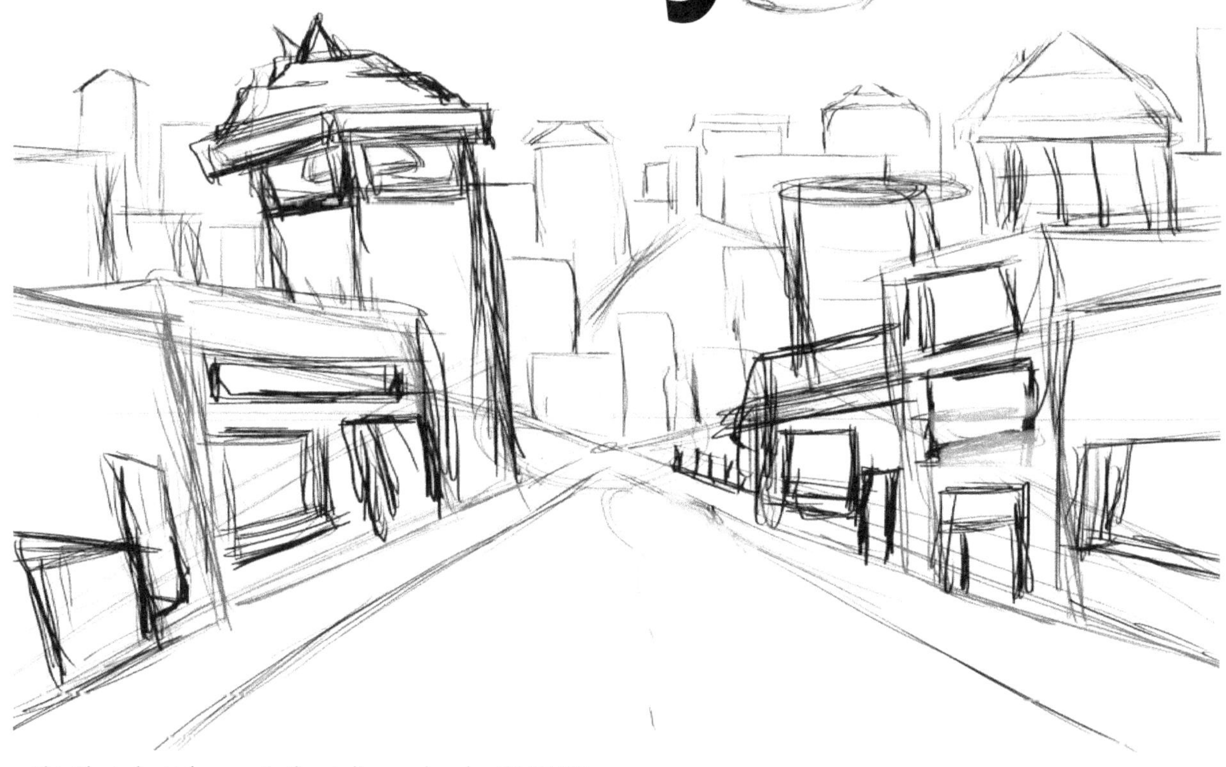

She would dream

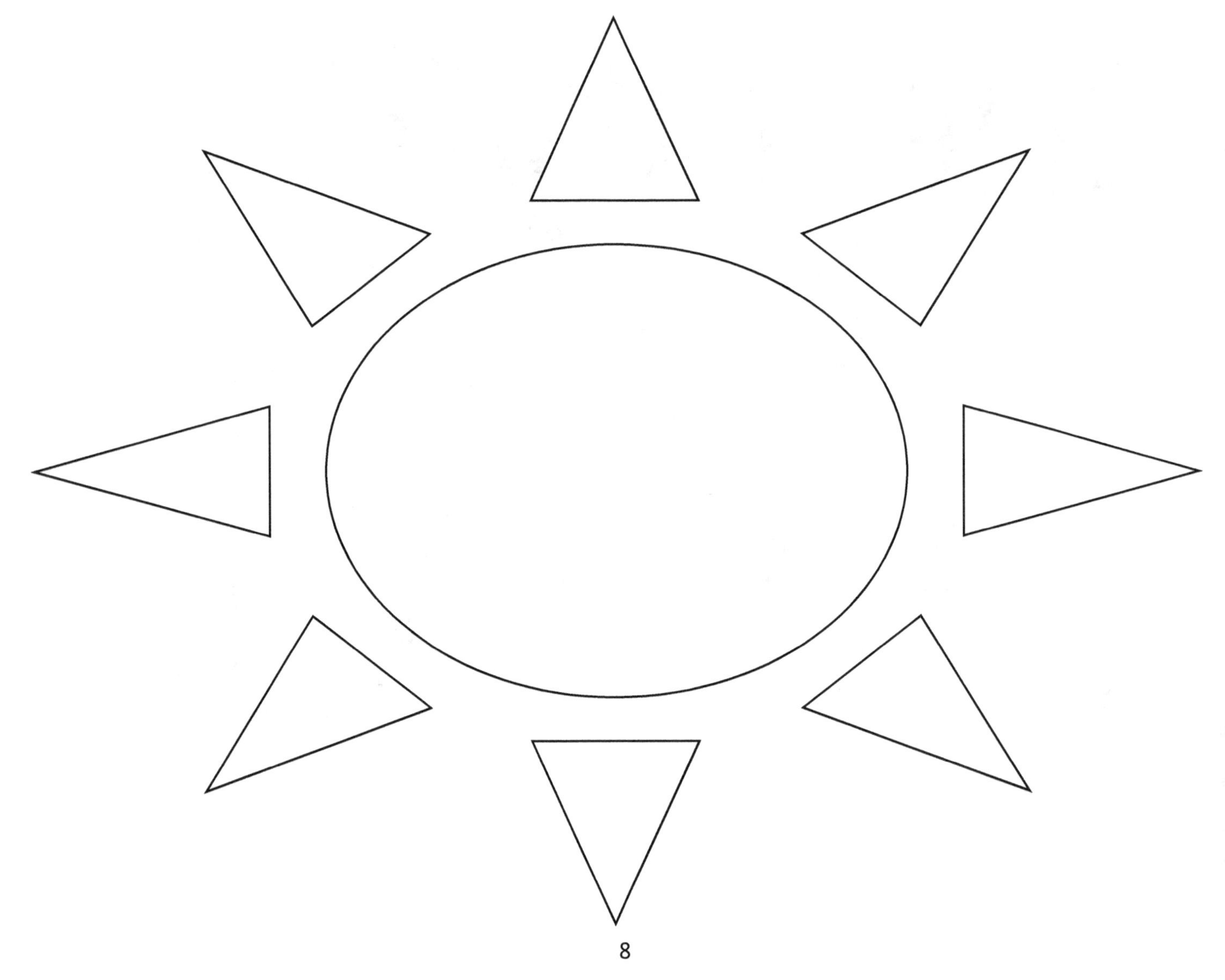

about

being

built

in

the city.

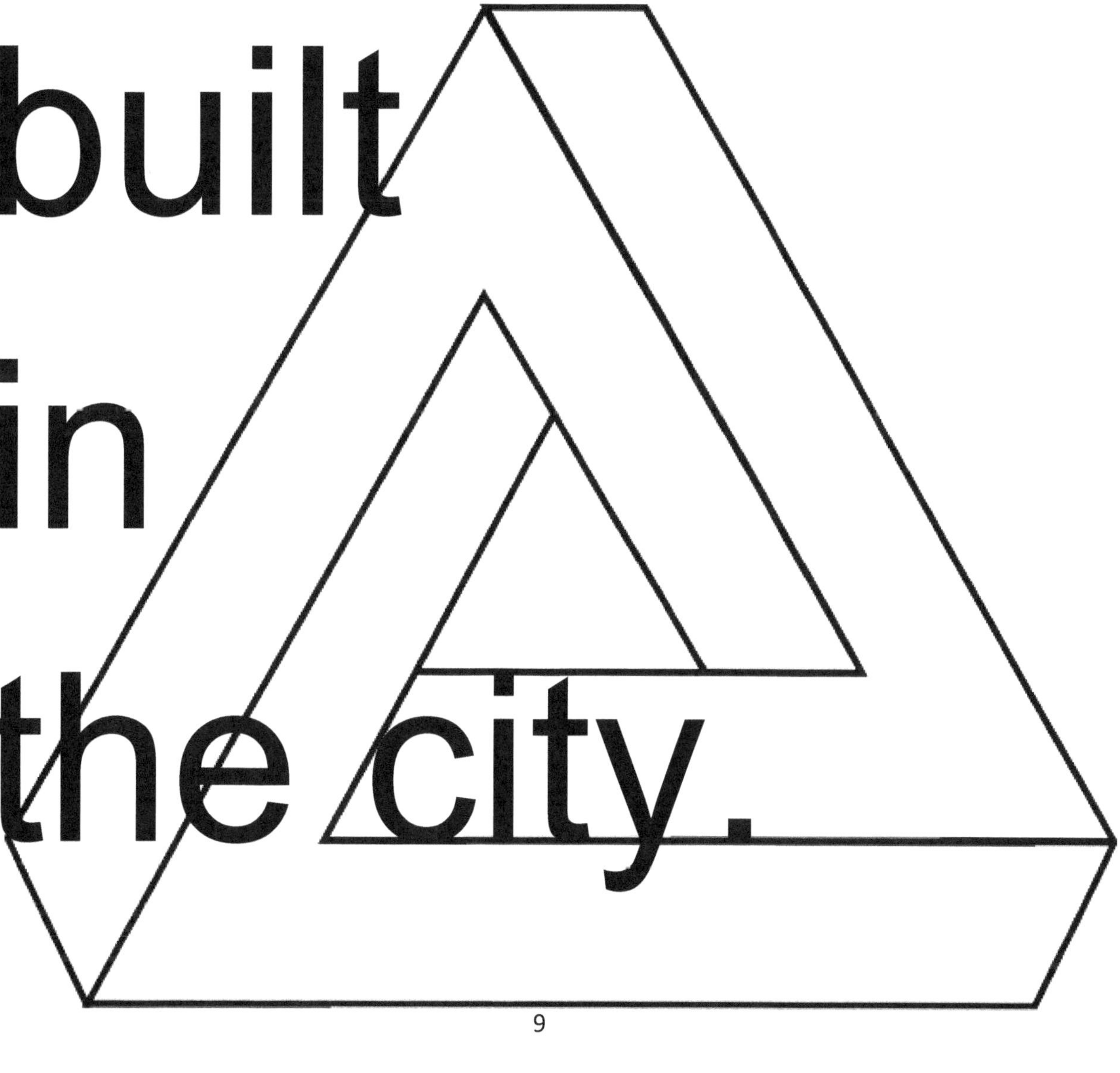

One day, people started to build up buildings

around the little house

Soon people stopped living

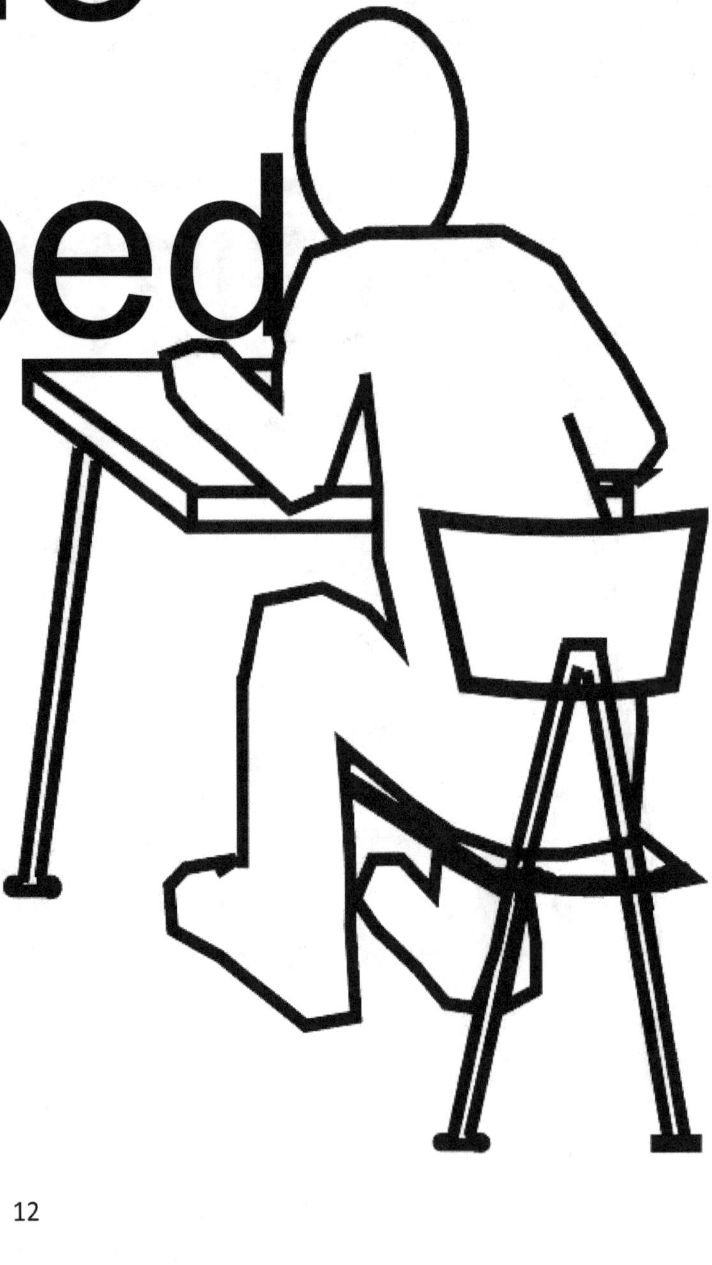

in that little house.

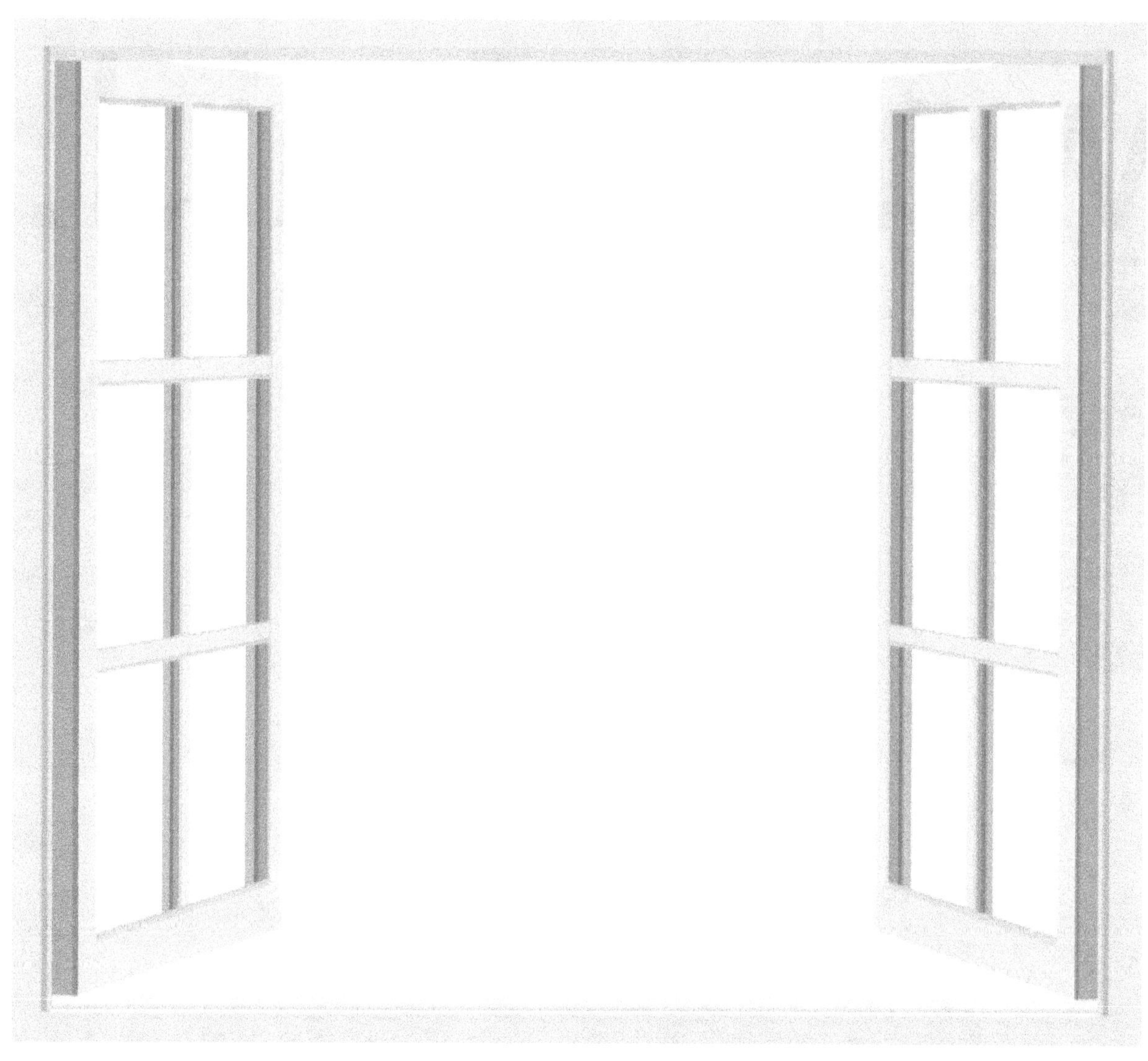

The little house was afraid.

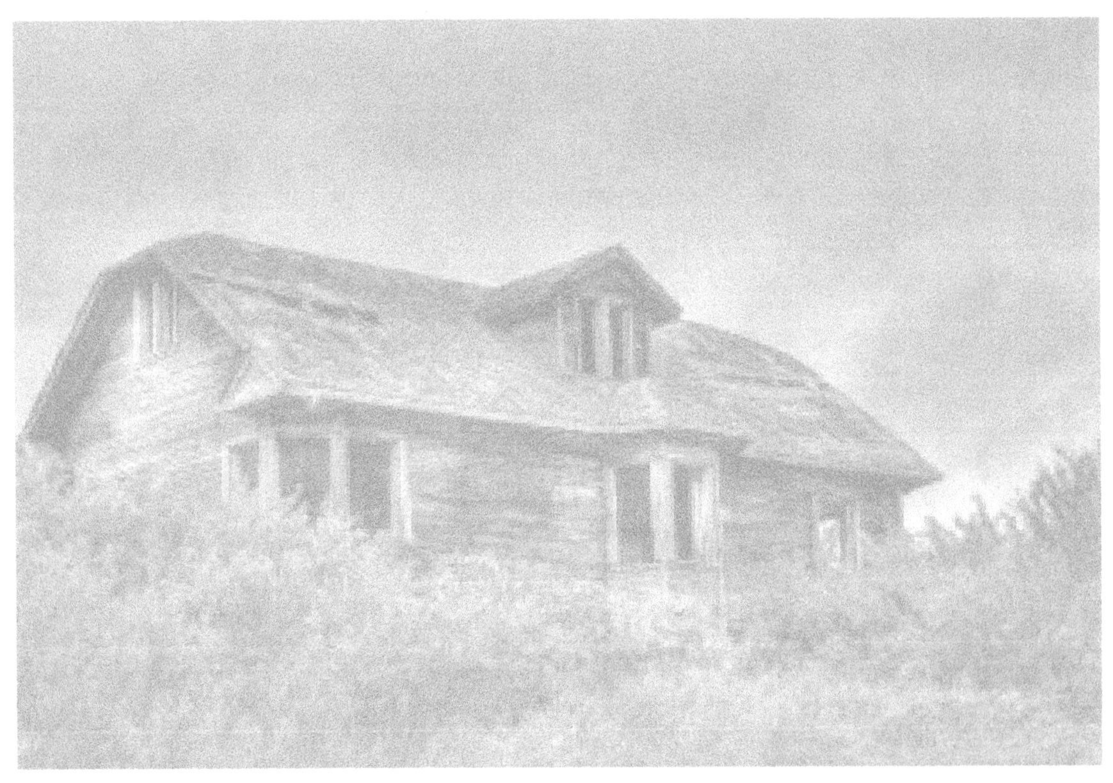

One day, a lady was walking by.

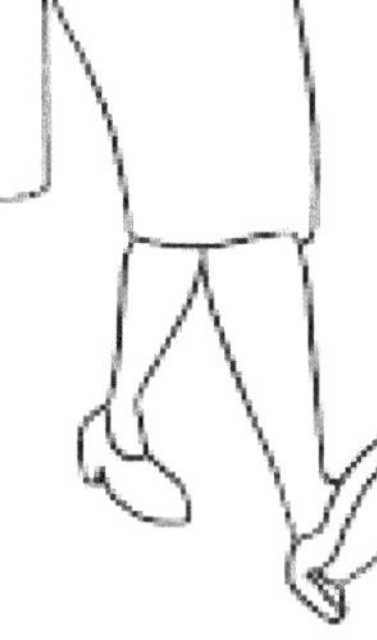

She said, “This is not right!”

“This little house does not belong here!”

“This little house does not belong here.”

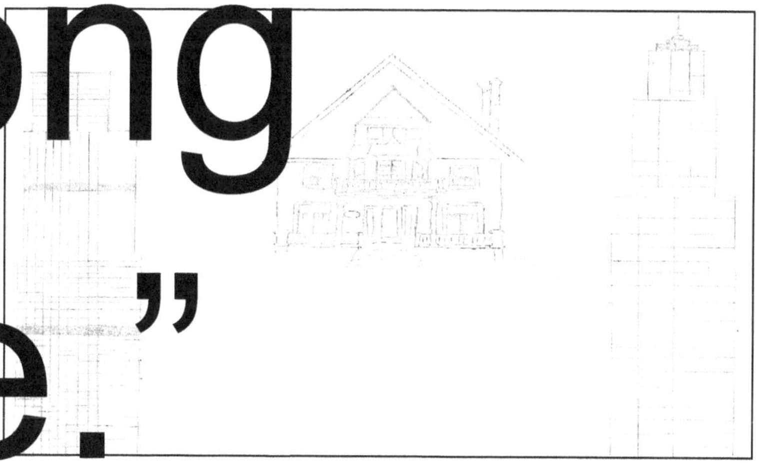

So, the lady took it to a place

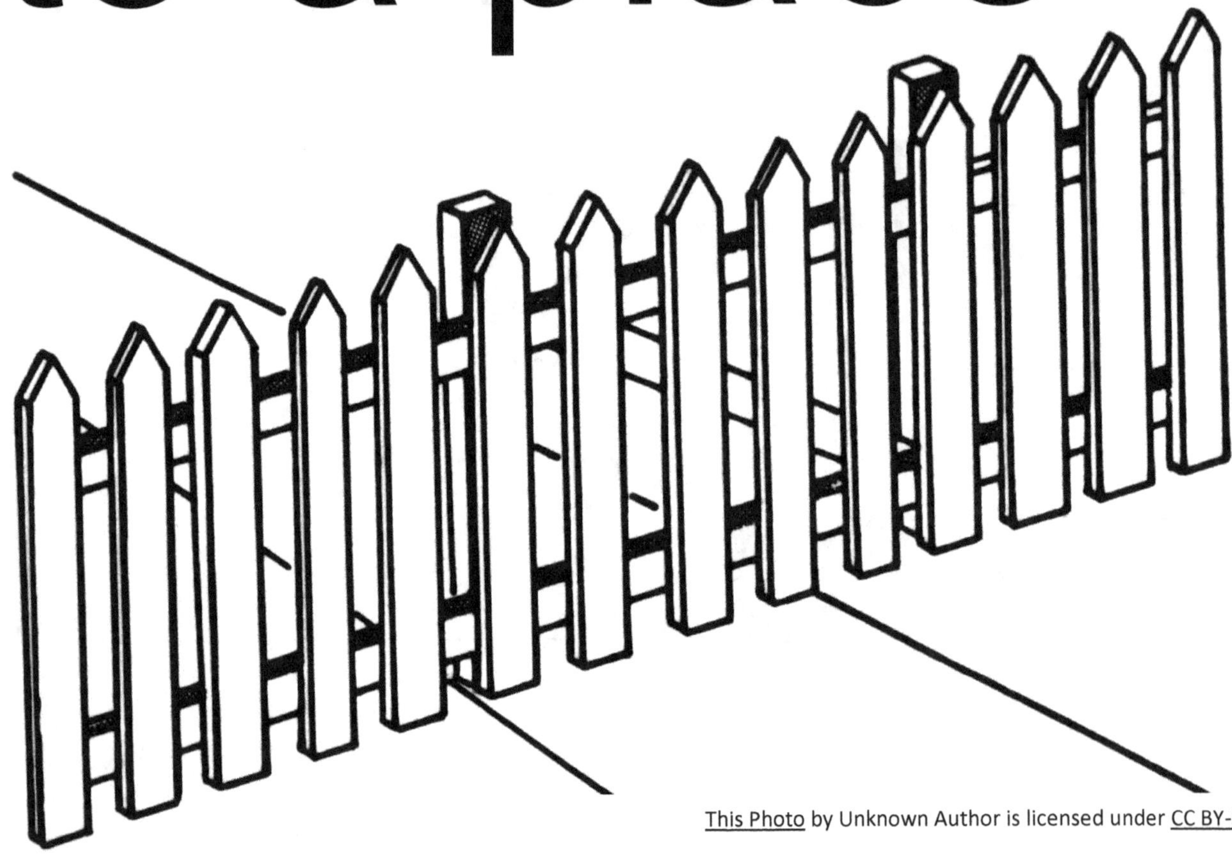

where it could be lived in,

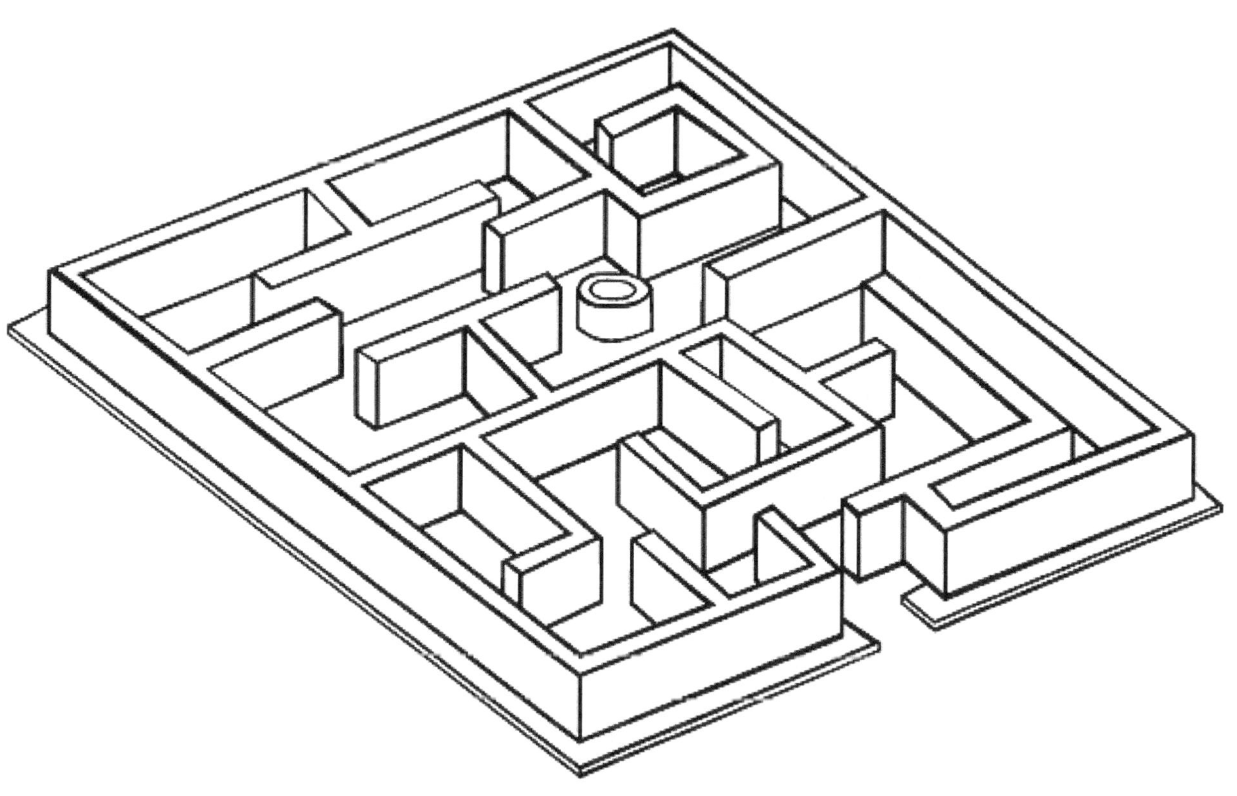

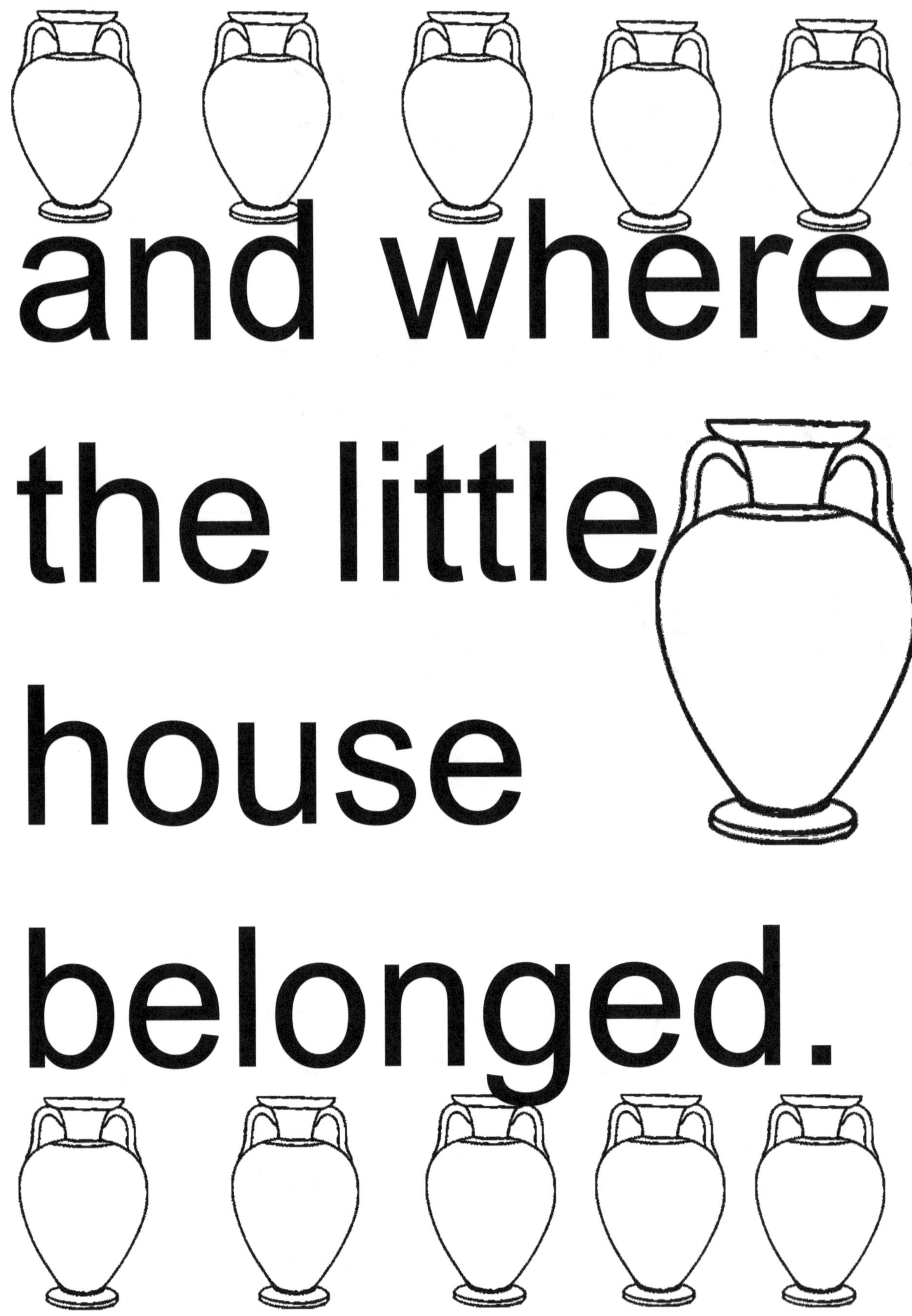

and where the little house belonged.

After that, the little house never dreamed

about going to the city ever again.

(A short story by *Dasia Carter*)

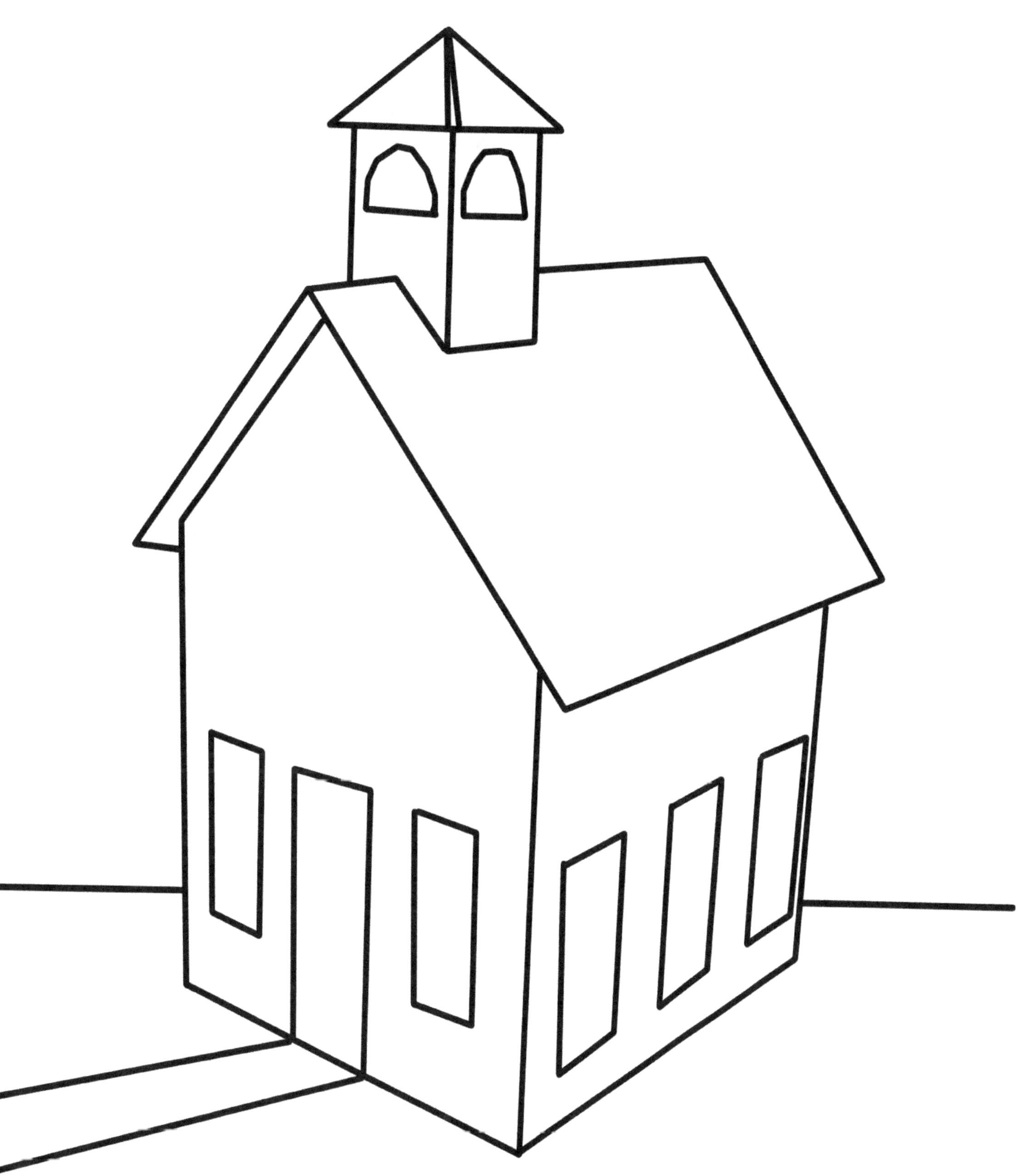

The "Little" House

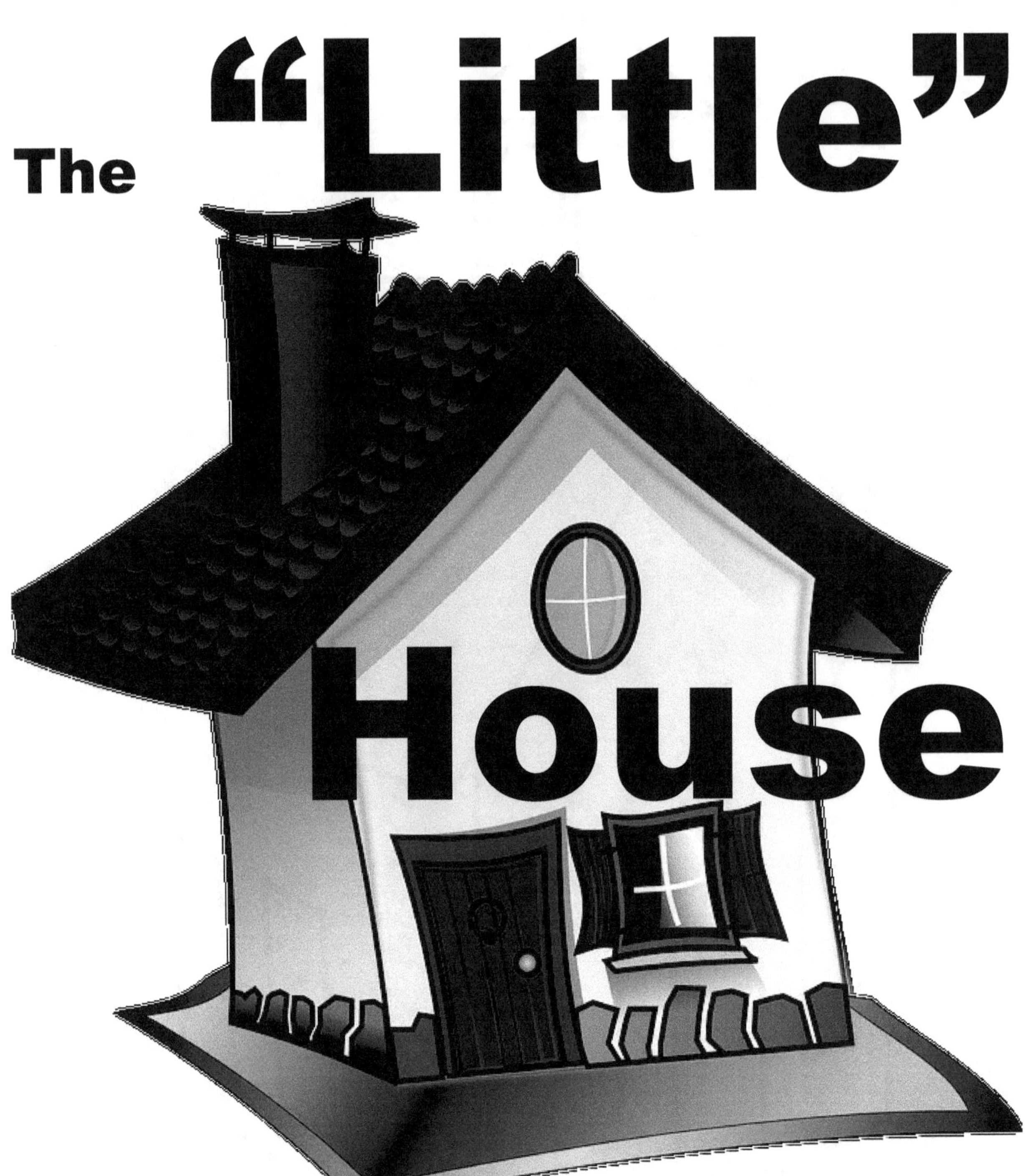

The Little House - A Coloring Book

Story by Dasia Carter

M.O.R.E. Publishers
Memphis, Tennessee
ISBN 978-0-9758549-8-3

www.ingramcontent.com/pod-product-compliance
Lightning Source LLC
LaVergne TN
LVHW061258100826
845148LV00008B/1173
* 9 7 8 0 9 7 5 8 5 4 9 8 3 *